This book belongs to:

_____

_____

Language consultant: Betty Root

This edition published by Parragon in 2009

Parragon
Chartist House
15-17 Trim Street
Bath BA1 1HA, UK
www.parragon.com

ISBN 978-1-4054-5023-2

Printed in China

I'm a Big Brother!

Written by Ronne Randall

Illustrated by Kristina Stephenson

Bath New York Singapore Hong Kong Cologne Delhi Melbourne

Luke was very excited. Grandma and Grandpa had been looking after him, but now Mommy and Daddy were home. And they had a wonderful surprise—a new baby!

"The baby is so tiny!" said Luke.
"You were this tiny once," said Daddy. "But now
you're big—you're Baby's big brother!"

"Can I play with Baby?" Luke asked.

"Soon," said Mommy. "But now Baby needs to sleep."

She put the baby in a crib. "This was yours when you were a baby," she told Luke.

"Babies need lots of sleep, because they have lots of growing to do," Mommy explained.
Luke looked into the crib. The baby was fast asleep.

"I'll wait until the baby wakes up," Luke thought.
"Then maybe we'll be able to play."

But the baby woke up, and was still too tiny
to play with Luke!

And the baby was still
too tiny to play
the next day,

and the day after,
and the day after that!

"You need to wait just a bit longer,"
Mommy or Daddy always said.

All Baby seemed to do was sleep or cry or eat,
or need a clean diaper.
"I wish Baby would hurry up and grow!"
Luke said every day.

One morning, when
Luke looked into
Baby's crib, Baby was
smiling—and
sitting up!
Luke was so excited
that he called Mommy and Daddy.
"Baby's getting bigger," they told Luke.

"Yes," said Mommy. "You were once as little as Baby, but you got big enough to play—and Baby will too!"

And Baby did start to grow.

Baby grew **bigger...**

and **bigger!**

Luke learned how to help dress Baby,

…and he even helped feed Baby.

"Baby is lucky to have a helpful big brother like you," said Daddy.

One afternoon, Mommy said to Luke,
"Let's take Baby to the park."

"Will Baby be able to play in the sandbox with me?
Or come on the swings?" Luke asked.

"Not just yet," said Mommy.
"But Baby would love to watch you! A big brother
can show Baby all sorts of things."

At the park, Luke rushed to the sandbox.
"I'll show Baby how to make
a sandcastle!" he said.
Baby watched happily while Luke
built a wonderful sandcastle.

"It's even more fun when Baby watches," Luke said.
"I think Baby is having fun too!" said Mommy.

That night, Mommy asked Luke, "Would you like to help me give Baby a bath?"

"Yes, please!" said Luke.

While Mommy washed Baby, Luke sailed a boat through the bubbles and made little splashes in the tub. Baby laughed and kicked and splashed too. It was lots of fun—almost like playing with Baby!

A few days later, Luke was playing with his train
in the living room. Suddenly, Baby crawled over
and grabbed the engine!
"Mommy! Daddy!" cried Luke. "Baby is taking my train!
Make Baby stop!"

"I think Baby is trying to tell you something,"
Mommy said, smiling at Luke.

"What?" Luke asked.
"I think," said Mommy, "that Baby is saying...
'I am ready to play with you now'!"

"Hooray!" cried Luke. He ran to the toybox
and picked up a soft, squishy ball.
"Catch!" said Luke, as he rolled the ball to Baby.

Baby laughed and tried
to catch the ball.

Luke rolled the ball
to Baby again, and this
time Baby grabbed it.

Baby laughed, and
Luke laughed too.
He rolled the ball to
Baby again and again.

"I think," Luke said to Mommy and Daddy,
"that being a big brother is going to be
LOTS of fun from now on!"

And it was!

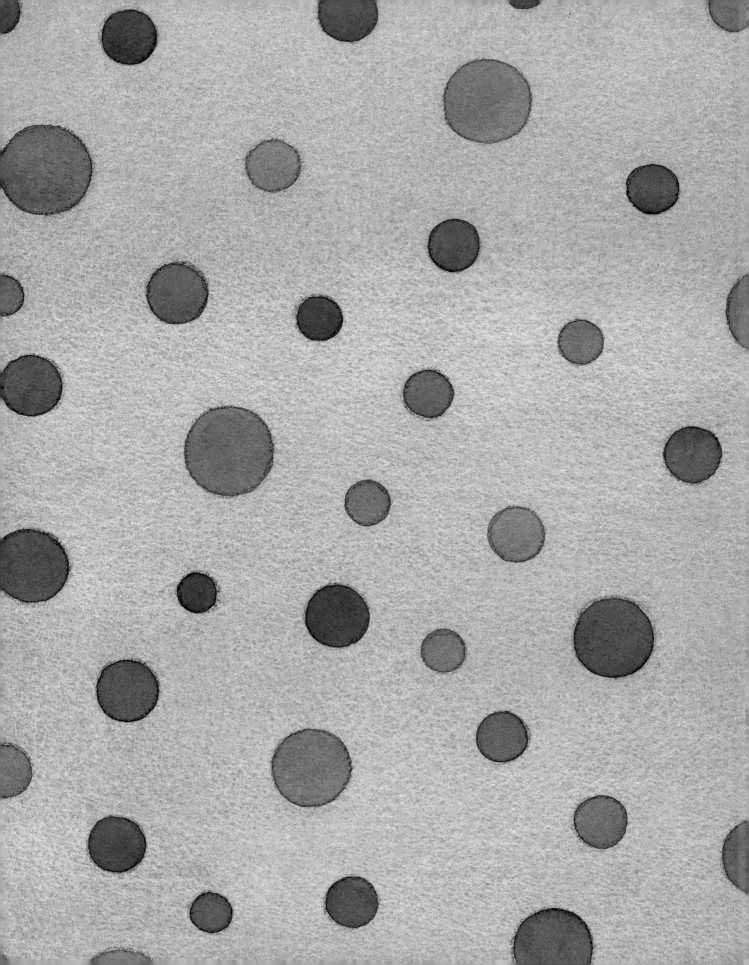